WELCOME TO
PASSPORT TO READING
A beginning reader's ticket to a brand-new world!

Every book in this program is designed to build read-along and read-alone skills, level by level, through engaging and enriching stories. As the reader turns each page, he or she will become more confident with new vocabulary, sight words, and comprehension.

These PASSPORT TO READING levels will help you choose the perfect book for every reader.

READING TOGETHER
Read short words in simple sentence structures together to begin a reader's journey.

READING OUT LOUD
Encourage developing readers to sound out words in more complex stories with simple vocabulary.

READING INDEPENDENTLY
Newly independent readers gain confidence reading more complex sentences with higher word counts.

READY TO READ MORE
Readers prepare for chapter books with fewer illustrations and longer paragraphs.

This book features sight words from the educator-supported Dolch Sight Words List. This encourages the reader to recognize commonly used vocabulary words, increasing reading speed and fluency.

For more information, please visit passporttoreadingbooks.com.

Enjoy the journey!

Little, Brown and Company

Hachette Book Group
237 Park Avenue, New York, NY 10017
Visit our website at lb-kids.com

Little, Brown and Company is a division of Hachette Book Group, Inc.
The Little, Brown name and logo are trademarks of Hachette Book Group, Inc.

The publisher is not responsible for websites (or their content) that are not owned by the publisher.

First Edition: February 2014
A Dozen Fairy Dresses originally published in May 2010
by Random House Children's Books, a division of Random House, Inc.
A Game of Hide-and-Seek originally published in January 2009
by Random House Children's Books, a division of Random House, Inc.
The Great Fairy Race and *The Fairy Berry Bake-Off* originally published in April 2008
by Random House Children's Books, a division of Random House, Inc.
Tink's Treasure Hunt originally published in August 2009
by Random House Children's Books, a division of Random House, Inc.

A Dozen Fairy Dresses, *A Game of Hide-and-Seek*, and *The Great Fairy Race* were written by Tennant Redbank and illustrated by the Disney Storybook Artists.

The Fairy Berry Bake-Off was written by Daisy Alberto and illustrated by the Disney Storybook Artists.

Tink's Treasure Hunt was written by Melissa Lagonegro and illustrated by Denise Shimabukuro, Jeff Clark, Merry Clingen, Adrienne Brown, Charles Pickens, and the Disney Storybook Artists.

ISBN 978-0-316-28329-8 (pb) — ISBN 978-0-316-40864-6 (paper over board)

10 9 8 7 6 5 4 3 2

WOR

Printed in the United States of America

Passport to Reading titles are leveled by independent reviewers applying the standards developed by Irene Fountas and Gay Su Pinnell in *Matching Books to Readers: Using Leveled Books in Guided Reading*, Heinemann, 1999.

Pixie Hollow
Reading Adventures

LITTLE, BROWN AND COMPANY
New York • Boston

A Dozen Fairy Dresses

L B

LITTLE, BROWN AND COMPANY

New York • Boston

Attention, Disney Fairies fans!
Look for these words
when you read this story.
Can you spot them all?

dresses

Lily

rose

clover

Queen Clarion has something to say.

"We will have a ball,"

Queen Clarion tells the fairies.

"It is Purple Moon Night."

Hem has a sewing talent.

She loves to make dresses.

She will make her own dress
for the ball.

All the fairies go to Hem.

"Will you make us dresses?"

asks Tinker Bell.

Hem does not have much time
to make all the dresses.
She flies back to her sewing room
very fast.

Next, Hem goes to see Lily.

Lily has a garden.

Hem wants to pick

flowers to use

on the dresses.

Lily and Hem pick a rose

for Rosetta.

They pick a daffodil

for Tinker Bell.

They choose a sweet pea
for Rani.

The clover is for Fawn.

Hem goes home.

She works all night long.

She sews a pink dress.

She adds ruffles to a green dress.

She sews on a flower.

She has two more dresses to make.

Hem is done!

She hangs up eleven dresses.

They are pretty!

The fairies come over

to see their dresses.

Each fairy loves her dress
and takes it home.

Hem rests on some petals.

She is tired.

Hem sits up.

She needs to get ready for the ball.

Hem does not have a new dress!

Hem looks in her closet.

She wishes

she had a new dress.

Hem is sad.

Hem has an idea!

She can use the petals.

Hem sews the petals

to one another.

It takes Hem all day
to make the dress.
She is happy with her work.

Hem flies to the ball
in her new dress.
Every fairy looks nice.
The ball is fun!

A Game of
Hide-and-Seek

L B

LITTLE, BROWN AND COMPANY
New York • Boston

Attention, Disney Fairies fans!
Look for these words
when you read this story.
Can you spot them all?

tulips

spiderweb

footprints

hedgehogs

Tinker Bell flies over the garden.

"Where are the fairies?" she asks.

Tink flies close to
some tall tulips.

She looks inside.

Rosetta is there!

The fairies play

hide-and-seek.

Tinker Bell looks

behind a spiderweb.

She looks under a pinecone.

She sees light
coming from a leaf.

It is Fira!

She glows like the sun.

Who will Tinker Bell find next?

Tink sees blue footprints

on a dirt path.

They lead to Bess!

Bess left the prints
when she hid.
She has blue paint
on her feet!

Tink finds Silvermist
behind a log.

Tink spots Fawn in a nest.

Iridessa is hiding with
the fireflies.

Nettle is in a cocoon.

Tinker Bell looks behind
a big rock.

Rani is there,

hiding by the pond.

Tink rests on a lily pad.

"Who is left?" she asks.

She needs to find

one more fairy.

Tink asks her friends
for help.
They look in the garden,
the mill, and the meadow.

Where can the

hidden fairy be?

Tink hears a snore.

The snore is coming from a log.

Inside the log are Beck

and some hedgehogs!

"Beck!" says Tinker Bell.

"Wake up!"

Beck yawns.

"You are the last one!" says Tink.

Beck is still sleepy.

She rolls over and
goes back to sleep.
Tinker Bell is tired, too.
The game of
hide-and-seek is over.
Now it is nap time!

The Great
Fairy Race

L B

LITTLE, BROWN AND COMPANY

New York • Boston

Attention, Disney Fairies fans!

Look for these words

when you read this story.

Can you spot them all?

frog

dove

balloon

snail

The fairy race has one rule.
The rule is that the first fairy
over the finish line wins!

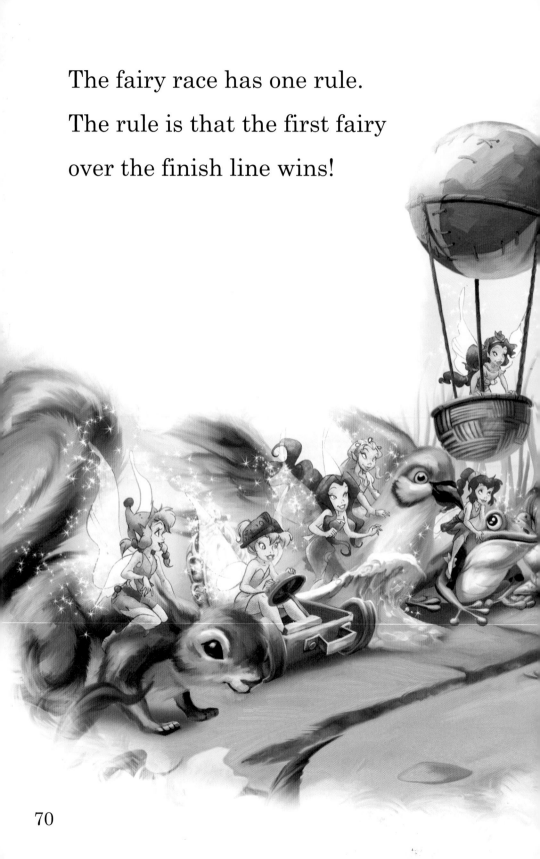

Fawn rides a frog.

Rani flies a dove.

Beck rides a squirrel.

Fira flies in a balloon.

Silvermist surfs on a wave.

Tinker Bell made a machine
to ride on.

Lily rides a big snail.

Bess sits in a wagon

pulled by a mouse.

The fairies race

one another!

They cross a river.

They pass a tree.

They go in the grass.

The race is very close.

The fairies are

wing and wing.

The fairies are almost
at the finish line.

Who will win?

Tinker Bell's machine
runs into Beck's squirrel.
They crash!
Tink and Beck are
out of the race!

Fawn and her frog

bump into Rani and her dove.

The dove hits
Fira's balloon.
The balloon sinks.

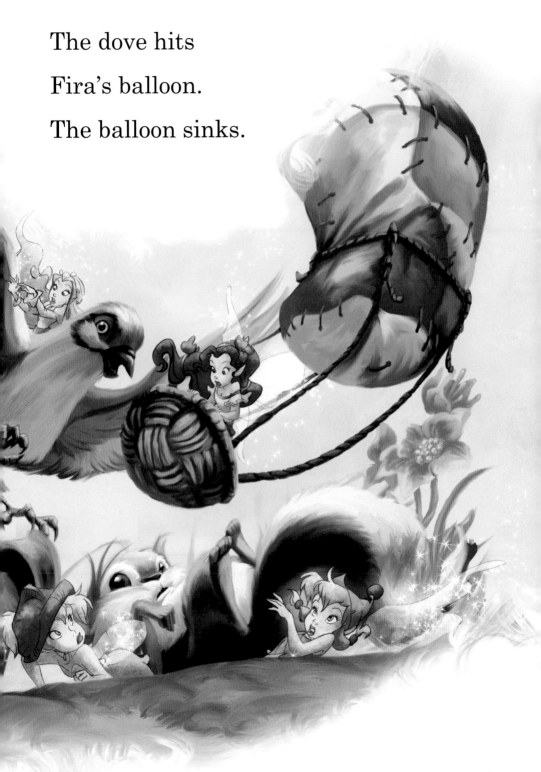

Bess and Silvermist

crash also.

They do not

finish the race.

Lily and her snail

go very slow.

They pass the others.

Lily and her snail
cross the finish line!
Lily wins the fairy race!

Queen Clarion says,

"Lily is the winner!"

The other fairies

join them.

In this race,

the slow snail

is the fastest animal!

The Fairy Berry Bake-Off

L B

LITTLE, BROWN AND COMPANY

New York • Boston

Attention, Disney Fairies fans!
Look for these words
when you read this story.
Can you spot them all?

flowers

chipmunk

cupcakes

muffins

The fairies

are hard at work

in Pixie Hollow.

Lily waters flowers.

Bess paints

in her house.

Silvermist picks up

drops of water.

Fira plays with

the fireflies.

Beck helps

a lost chipmunk.

Tinker Bell fixes

a broken pan.

The fairies want food
after working so hard.
They go to the bakery
to eat.

"I wonder what
the baking fairies
baked today," Lily says.

Dulcie is stirring

berries for a tart

over the stove.

Ginger is baking a tart, too.

Ginger gets mad at Dulcie.

"We cannot bake the same treat!"

says Ginger.

"I am sorry," says Dulcie.

"We can both bake tarts.

The other fairies

can choose the best one!"

"Fine," Ginger says.

"We will have a

fairy berry bake-off!"

Dulcie and Ginger
go back to baking.
They will start with
chocolate cake.

Next, they bake blueberry custard
and blackberry cupcakes.

"Yum!" Tink says.

"All these sweets

taste so good."

Ginger and Dulcie are mad.

They each want their dessert

to be the best one.

But the fairies love

all the treats!

"Try my muffins," says Dulcie.

"How about a honey bun?"

asks Ginger.

Tink does not know what to do.

There are so many sweets!

The cakes start
to fill the table.

Still, the fairies agree
that both Ginger's and Dulcie's
treats are tasty!

In the kitchen,

Dulcie and Ginger

bake their final cakes.

They spot the last berry

and both want to use it.

"It is mine," says Ginger.

"No, it is mine!" says Dulcie.

They both pull on the berry!

Dulcie falls back,

right into her cake!

Ginger falls back, too.

The cakes are smashed.

Tink walks in to check on them.

As she enters the kitchen,

a cupcake lands on her head.

Dulcie and Ginger

look at the mess they made.

Cake and cupcakes

are everywhere!

Tinker Bell is mad.

"The berry bake-off is over,"

Tink says.

"You are both great bakers!"

Dulcie and Ginger blush.

"We are both great bakers!"

says Dulcie.

"Try baking together!"
says Tink.

Dulcie and Ginger agree
that is a great idea.

Ginger and Dulcie
bake the perfect cake.
Everyone agrees it is
the best one!

Tink's Treasure Hunt

LITTLE, BROWN AND COMPANY
New York • Boston

Attention, Disney Fairies fans!
Look for these words
when you read this story.
Can you spot them all?

Terence

mirror

firefly

trolls

Terence and Tinker Bell
are best friends.
Terence is a dust-keeper fairy.

In Pixie Hollow,

dust-keeper fairies

make magic pixie dust.

Terence and Tinker Bell like
to build things together.
They make a good team.

Terence likes

to give Tink advice.

"Steady," Terence says.

Tink gets mad.

"Go away!" Tink says.

That night, Tink goes to
the Fairy-Tale Theater.
The show is about
a magic mirror.
The mirror
can grant one wish!
It can be found
on a faraway island.

Tink wants to find
the magic mirror!
She draws a map
of where she will go.

Next, Tinker Bell

makes a balloon.

She works very hard.

The balloon is done!

Tink hops in and flies away.

It is nighttime,

and Tink is hungry.

All her food is gone!

Blaze, a firefly, ate all the food.

It is dark, but Blaze can help Tink!

He shines his light

so Tinker Bell can see her map.

They land
and find a ship.
Tink must go inside.

Tink and Blaze

enter the dark ship.

Blaze lights the way.

Down a path
are two trolls.
Tink and Blaze
sneak past them.

At the other end of the path,

they find the magic mirror!

"I wish," Tink says.

Blaze buzzes in her ear.

"I wish you would be quiet!"

Tink yells.

Blaze stops buzzing.

"Oh no!" Tink says.

Tink used her one wish.

"I wish Terence was here,"

Tink says.

Then she sees Terence

in the mirror.

Terence has found Tink!

He is on the ship.

Tink is so happy to see him.

The two friends hug.

Suddenly,

rats are all around them!

Terence makes a big shadow

and scares away the rats.

Tink and Terence escape!
They find the balloon
and fly back home.
They are happy
to be together again.

Tink, Terence, and Blaze

are glad to be such special friends.

THE END!

Read more
Disney Fairies adventures
coming soon!

Adventure at Skull Rock

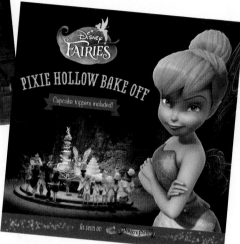

PIXIE HOLLOW BAKE OFF

Cupcake toppers included!

As seen on PIRATE FAIRY

Wake Up, Croc!

PIRATE FAIRY

Over 80 stickers included!

Reusable Sticker Book

CHECKPOINTS IN THIS BOOK ✓

A Dozen Fairy Dresses

WORD COUNT	GUIDED READING LEVEL	NUMBER OF DOLCH SIGHT WORDS
253	I	169

A Game of Hide-and-Seek

WORD COUNT	GUIDED READING LEVEL	NUMBER OF DOLCH SIGHT WORDS
230	H	135

The Great Fairy Race

WORD COUNT	GUIDED READING LEVEL	NUMBER OF DOLCH SIGHT WORDS
194	G	107

The Fairy Berry Bake-Off

WORD COUNT	GUIDED READING LEVEL	NUMBER OF DOLCH SIGHT WORDS
357	J	207

Tink's Treasure Hunt

WORD COUNT	GUIDED READING LEVEL	NUMBER OF DOLCH SIGHT WORDS
313	K	186